Jane gave to her bunny
Things to do him good.
Carrots, turnips, cabbage —
Everything she should.

But poor Ronnie longed for
What he couldn't get.
Something that his mistress
Never gave her pet.

Ronnie had a weakness,
Filled his heart with grief.
What he longed to nibble —
Dandelion leaf!

In the neighbour's garden,
Dandelions grew.
He could have a feast there,
Ronnie Rabbit knew.

Now turn to the back of the book.

Printed and Published by D. C. Thomson & Co., Ltd., Dundee and London.

Dear Girls,

Here is another great Twinkle Book specially for you.

Hilda Hen, The yellow balloon, The King's new castle and Busy Bee are just some of the super stories you will find inside.

You'll also enjoy reading about your favourite "Twinkle" friends ~ Nurse Nancy, Sam, My Baby Brother, Patch and Elfie.

There are lots of interesting puzzles to do, too~and an exciting game to play!

Love from,
Twinkle.

The Christmas foal

"CHRISTMAS is coming. The goose is getting fat. Please put a penny in the old man's hat . . ." sang Anna, as she helped Daddy to mix Snowflake's oats.

"When is Snowflake's foal going to be born?" asked Anna, lovingly patting her white pony.

"Any day now, dear," said Daddy, giving Snowflake a bucket of oats.

2 — "Can I give Snowflake her Christmas present?" Anna asked. "I know it's only Christmas Eve, but it's so cold."

"I think that's a good idea," said Daddy, smiling. Anna rushed into the house and came out with the brightly coloured horse blanket she had knitted.

"Here you are, Snowflake. This will keep you warm while you wait for your foal to arrive," she said.

3 — The snow began to fall quite heavily as Anna and her daddy finished settling down Snowflake for the night.

Anna left the stable yard and turned to say "goodnight" to Snowflake. The moon was shining brightly over the stable, and Anna thought it looked just like a Christmas card picture.

"I hope the foal is born tonight," said Anna. "It would be exciting."

When they reached the house, Mummy was busy in the kitchen.

"Oh, good! Tea and toast," said Daddy, rubbing his hands together.

4 — "Mm, just what we need to warm us up," said Anna.

Mummy carried the tray of tea into the living room.

"When I was young, we used to sing carols in the village square, and dance around the Christmas tree on Christmas Eve," said Mummy. "Mrs Brown would bring us all hot drinks and mince pies and Mr Penbroke, the blacksmith, would roast chestnuts for us ."

Anna enjoyed listening to her mother's stories about the wonderful Christmases past. But she had a feeling in her heart that this would be a special Christmas.

5 — "When Anna awoke on Christmas morning, the air seemed to buzz with excitement. Anna took her stocking, now bulging with presents, downstairs to the kitchen.

"Merry Christmas, dear," said Mummy, as she cooked breakfast.

"Where is Daddy?" Anna said, realising he wasn't in the room.

"I'm here" said Daddy as he came in the back door. "Merry Christmas."

"Is everything alright?" asked Mummy.

"Yes, dear. I'm pleased to tell you Snowflake has had a strong, healthy foal." said Daddy.

6 — "Oh, Daddy. That's wonderful! When did she have it? What colour is it?" Anna couldn't stop asking questions.

Sipping a cup of tea, Daddy told Anna that Snowflake had a son and that he was a rich chestnut brown colour.

Anna dressed quickly. The Christmas presents, which usually she couldn't wait to open, lay for the moment forgotten. Her only thoughts were of Snowflake and her foal.

"Oh, Snowflake, he's beautiful!" sighed Anna, as she entered the stable. The new foal nuzzled her hand for a second before he returned to his mother's side.

7 — "What are you going to call him?" asked Daddy.

"I don't know," said Anna. "It will have to be a special name as he was born on Christmas night."

On Christmas evening, after all the presents had been opened, Anna and her parents sat around their open log fire.

"Let's roast some chestnuts," said Daddy.

8 —"That's it, Daddy! That's just the name for Snowflake's foal!"

"What is?" asked Daddy.

"Chestnut! It will be a lovely name. He is chestnut colour, and he was born at Christmas when we eat chestnuts," said Anna.

"Chestnut," repeated Daddy. "Yes, dear. That is a lovely name."

Nancy the little nurse

1 — One morning, Nancy's friend, Tim, brought a broken sledge to the Dollies Hospital. Mr Jingle fixed it at once, so Tim could go sledging that day.

2 — Tim asked Mr Jingle if Nancy could come to the park with him, as the Hospital wasn't busy. Mr Jingle said, "Yes!" Nancy quickly put on her warm clothes and boots.

3 — Tim also took his dog, Scamp, to the park. "Scamp enjoys playing in the snow," said Tim. Nancy noticed her friends, the twins, Lucy and Ruth, in the park.

4 — Nancy was worried when she saw that Lucy and Ruth had brought their dollies sledging. "I hope their dolls don't have an accident," sighed Nancy.

5 — Nancy, Tim and Scamp had a super afternoon, playing in the snowy park. As they were leaving, Nancy and Tim heard the twins shouting for help.

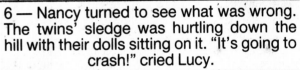

6 — Nancy turned to see what was wrong. The twins' sledge was hurtling down the hill with their dolls sitting on it. "It's going to crash!" cried Lucy.

7 — Nancy ran to stop the sledge, but she was too late. The sledge smashed into a tree at the foot of the hill and the dolls fell off. The twins *were* upset.

8 — "We don't have an ambulance to take the dolls to the Hospital," sighed Nancy. Then she had an idea. "Tie the rope of your sledge to Scamp's collar," she told Tim.

OUT PATIENTS
SURGERY HOURS
9 am — 6 pm

You can colour this picture with your paints or crayons.

9 — Nancy laid the twins' dolls on Tim's sledge. Then Scamp pulled the sledge to the Dollies Hospital. "Grandad will mend your dolls," Nancy told the twins.

10 — Mr Jingle *was* surprised when he saw the "sledge ambulance" arriving at the Hospital. "Scamp looks just like a husky pulling an Eskimo sledge," he smiled.

Meet Nurse Nancy in "Twinkle", on sale every Wednesday.

Fairytale puzzles

Colour this picture of Rumpelstiltskin with your paints or crayons, then try to find six hidden bobbins.

Which plait of Rapunzel's hair leads to the prince?

Answer - B

Lead Little Red Riding Hood through the maze to Grandma's cottage.

Can you spot six differences between these two pictures of the Sleeping Beauty?

Hilda Hen

1 — When Hilda the white hen arrived at Primrose Farm, she flapped her wings. "I wish I was still at my old farm," she said and sighed unhappily. "I feel lonely."

2 — Hilda looked into the hen–house. "Where am I supposed to sit?" she demanded rudely. No one answered, because she was so bad tempered.

3 — Hilda marched outside to see Charlie the cockerel. "There's no room in that hen house," she moaned. "And all the other hens are red. I don't like it here."

4 — "I'll find you a space in the hen house," said Charlie. But then Valerie, the farmer's daughter, scattered corn for the hens. Charlie dashed off for lunch.

5 — "Some help *you* are," thought Hilda. "I'll find a place for my nest myself." Hilda went into the pony's field. "Can I build a nest here?" she asked. "Yes," replied the pony.

6 — Next morning, Valerie and her mummy got a surprise when they saw Hilda. "Please don't disturb her," said Mummy. "She's sitting on her eggs."

7 — Hilda sat on her eggs all day. By evening, she felt hungry, so she went for something to eat. Suddenly, Charlie saw some magpies flying above Hilda's nest.

8 — Hilda and Charlie raced over to save the eggs. "Go away," Hilda clucked angrily. "You're not getting my eggs." Hilda sat down on her eggs and shielded them.

9 — Hilda sat tightly on her nest while Charlie flapped his wings and squawked loudly at the magpies. The magpies flew off. "Thank you, Charlie," said Hilda.

10 — Valerie had seen what had happened and ran to fetch her daddy. The farmer came and moved Hilda's nest into the hen house. "It's best," said Charlie.

11 — When Hilda settled down in the hen house, she found that the other hens were quite friendly after all. "We didn't speak because you were rude," they said.

12 — "I'm sorry," apologised Hilda. Hilda sat on her eggs until she heard them crack. "My eggs are hatching!" she cried. The hens crowded round to watch.

13 — Hilda's chicks hatched quickly. "They're beautiful!" cried the hens. "And they look just like you, Hilda." Hilda *was* pleased. "I'm going to like living here after all," she thought.

A job for Farrah

IN Bramble Wood, there lived a lazy, little fairy, named Farrah. Farrah was also very naughty, so she was always in trouble.

One day, the Fairy Queen ordered Farrah to come and see her.

"You need to learn to behave yourself, Farrah," said the Fairy Queen, "so I'm giving you a job to keep you out of mischief."

The Fairy Queen told Farrah about the forester, Mr Willow, and his wife, who lived in a cottage in the woods.

"They've got a baby now, so Mrs Willow needs a little extra help around the house," explained the Fairy Queen. "I want *you* to help the family as much as you can."

So Farrah flew to the Willows' cottage. But, instead of working, Farrah sat outside, sulking. She didn't want to look after a baby or do housework.

Just then, Mrs Willow came out of the cottage and put her baby in a pram.

"Sleep quietly, Sarah," Mrs Willow whispered to the baby, "and I can wash the clothes in peace."

"So Mrs Willow wants peace and quiet!" thought Farrah, with a smirk.

Farrah was beginning to feel mischievous. She decided to play a trick or two on Mrs Willow.

The naughty fairy flew over to the baby and tickled her under the chin. The baby woke suddenly and began crying. Mrs Willow came rushing out of the cottage to comfort her.

"I'll never get my washing done, now that you're awake, Sarah," sighed Mrs Willow.

Farrah should have felt sorry for her trick, but, instead, she just laughed.

Later that day, Mrs Willow *did* manage to wash the laundry. But, when she hung it on the line and went back indoors, Farrah pulled the clothes pegs out. All the clothes fell to the ground.

And so it went on. Farrah carried on playing naughty tricks, day and night.

One evening, Farrah turned on the kitchen taps and let the water overflow on to the floor.

Farrah hid behind a flower pot and giggled. Mr and Mrs Willow didn't find it funny, of course. In fact, they were tired and fed up with the strange "accidents". The next morning, they packed their suitcases and left the cottage.

At first, Farrah enjoyed having the cottage to herself. Soon, however, the little fairy found that she missed the family. Farrah suddenly felt very sorry for all her tricks. She hadn't realised the cottage would be so lonely without the family.

"It's my fault they've gone away," sobbed Farrah. "If only they'd come back, I'd help them all the time."

"Do you *really* mean that, Farrah?" asked a voice.

It was the Fairy Queen. She smiled at Farrah.

"If you make up for all the bad things you've done, I'll cast a magic spell and bring the family back," the Fairy Queen said. "You could start by cleaning the cottage from top to bottom."

So Farrah flitted around for a whole week, cleaning, scrubbing, dusting and polishing. The Fairy Queen *was* impressed.

"As you've worked so hard, I'll make the family return," she said.

Farrah *was* pleased when the family came back, that afternoon. And Mrs Willow was delighted when she saw her sparkling home.

"There must be a good fairy living here," she joked.

Mrs Willow didn't know how true this was!

That evening, Farrah settled down to sleep beside the baby.

"I'll never be naughty again," she thought, happily.

The Fairy Queen felt pleased, too. She had changed Farrah into a good fairy, without even casting a spell.

It was lucky that Farrah didn't know the family had only been away on holiday!

The yellow balloon

THE yellow balloon was the only balloon left hanging outside Mr Peters' toyshop.

"I wish someone would buy me," he sighed.

He had no sooner said this when a little girl came along.

"Ooh, look, Grandma!" she cried. "A yellow balloon. Can I have it, please?"

"Yes, Mandy," replied Grandma with a smile.

Mr Peters came out to untie the yellow balloon. But then a gust of wind snatched the balloon from his hand. The wind carried the balloon high over the city. At last, the wind dropped and the balloon felt himself falling. His long string caught in the branches of a tree. He tugged and tugged, but it was no use. He was stuck. Luckily a friendly thrush freed him.

"Thank you!" cried the yellow balloon as, once again, the wind carried him into the air.

After a while, the yellow balloon floated over a school playground. It was play-time and all the children were outside.

"Look!" cried one girl. "What a lovely, yellow balloon. Let's try to catch it."

The children jumped up at the yellow balloon, but they couldn't catch him, no matter how hard they tried.

"Phew!" gasped the yellow balloon. "That was close! I didn't fancy belonging to *all* those children."

The wind blew the balloon away from the school and over the town.

By this time it was getting dark. The yellow balloon was quite tired. He was glad when the wind stopped blowing and he landed gently in a garden. The yellow balloon was nearly asleep when a light snapped on.

"There's something in our garden," said a lady's voice.

"Let's go and take a look," replied her husband.

"Oh, dear!" thought the yellow balloon. "What's going to happen to me?"

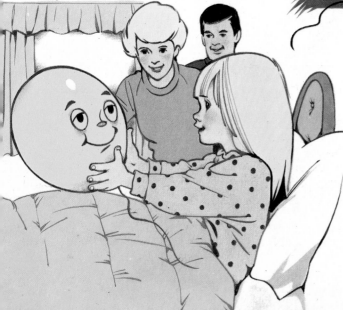

The yellow balloon needn't have worried, because the people were pleased to see him.

"A yellow balloon!" cried the lady. "Wonderful! Now Mandy will have her yellow birthday balloon after all!"

The lady tied the balloon to the end of her daughter's bed. The little girl *was* pleased to see the yellow balloon in the morning.

"It's just like the balloon grandma was going to buy for me!" she cried.

The yellow balloon was very happy. "Wasn't I clever to find my way to Mandy's house," he smiled.

Elfie

Elfie is a tiny elf who lives in a tree-stump house in the magic woods. He is friendly with all the woodland folk and always has lots of fun.

1 — It had snowed in the magic woods during the night. Elfie's cousin, Peter Pixie, hurried over to Elfie's house, pulling his sledge. "Let's go sledging!" he called.

2 — Everyone was sledging. They were having great fun. "Watch me!" yelled Peter, as he hurtled down the slope. "You'll crash!" wailed Elfie.

3 — Sure enough, Peter *did* crash. He hit a tree-stump and his sledge smashed into bits. Luckily, Peter wasn't hurt. "You won't be able to sledge now," sighed Elfie.

4 — As Elfie picked up the broken sledge, he had an idea. "These bits look like skis," he said. "Let's try them out." "Ooh, yes!" cheered Peter.

5 — Elfie fetched some string and tied his feet and Peter's on to the strips of wood. "I can't wait to try!" laughed Peter.

6 — The skis were a great success. Elfie and Peter skied around the woods until it was tea-time. "Come on!" cheered Elfie. "I'll race you home." "What a super day this has been," smiled Peter. "I'm glad I broke my sledge!"

Sally's winter store

1 — Sally Squirrel was going to hide her winter store of nuts. The kind squirrel had even gathered *extra* nuts for any other squirrels who might need them.

2 — Sally wanted to hide her nuts in the hollow tree where she had always kept her winter store. But a lumberjack had sawn it down to use as firewood.

3 — "I'll hide my nuts under some leaves, instead," thought Sally. But she changed her mind when she saw two children kicking the leaves as they ran along.

4 — Sally decided to store her nuts in the blue-tits' old house in Mr Gray's garden. But it wasn't there! "Mr Gray has taken it away to paint," explained Robbie Robin.

5 — "I'll *never* find a place to hide my winter store," sighed Sally. "You could hide your nuts in my old nest," suggested Robbie, pointing his wing. "It's over there."

6 — Robbie showed Sally his old nest under Mr Gray's hedge. "Your store will be safe here," said Robbie, as he helped Sally to put her nuts into the nest.

7 — Just then, Mr Gray and his children, Peter and Penny, came out into the garden, to plant some bulbs in front of the hedge. Peter found Robbie's old nest.

8 — Mr Gray told Peter he could have the nest, as Robbie didn't live in it any more. So Peter took the nest with Sally's nuts still inside it. "Oh, dear!" gasped Robbie.

9 — Poor Sally didn't need to find a place to hide her winter store now, because she didn't have any nuts to hide. She *did* feel sad. "Whatever will I do?" she sighed.

10 — The following day, Robbie Robin visited Sally. "You needn't worry about your winter store, Sally," he said, mysteriously. "I've got a surprise for you!"

11 — Robbie led Sally to a group of her squirrel chums. They had all collected extra nuts and hidden them in an old copper kettle, especially for Sally.

12 — Sally *was* surprised! "You've always stored away extra nuts, in case we needed them," explained Sammy Squirrel, "so, *this* year, *we* collected extra nuts for *you*."

Patch

Paula Perkins has a cute, little kitten called Patch and she loves him very much. Patch likes to join in with everything Paula does.

1 — One day, Paula and Patch were at a Christmas party. They were having great fun playing lots of party games. Suddenly, Patch realised that Paula had disappeared.

2 — Patch was looking for Paula, when someone came into the room. "It's Santa!" cried the children. Patch thought there was something odd about Santa.

3 — Patch went over to Santa and sniffed around his feet. The little kitten lifted Santa's trouser leg. "Santa has wooden legs!" cried the children in amazement.

4 — Patch then jumped up on to Santa's shoulder and pulled off his beard. "You've spoiled the game," cried "Santa". "Santa" had been Paula all the time!

5 — Paula had dressed up and stood on stilts to make herself look taller. "You fooled us!" laughed her friends. "But not Patch. He's too clever!"

Before you play this fun filled game, either trace or cut out these four elf counters.

Roll a dice and throw a six to start. Then, next throw, off you go.

All along the track you'll come across obstacles and helpful rewards.

The winner is the first player to reach Santa's sack. Good luck!

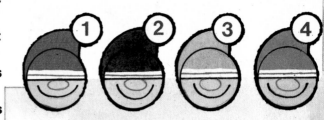

22 Leave out food for the birds. Go on two spaces.

23

24

25

21

20

26 Stop to have a snowball fight. Go back two spaces.

19 Stop to listen to carol singers. Miss a go.

27

18

28

17

16 Polish the reindeers' sleighbells. Go on two spaces.

29 Take a lazy shortcut across skating pond. Slip and slide back two spaces.

Finish

A Treat for Tootsie

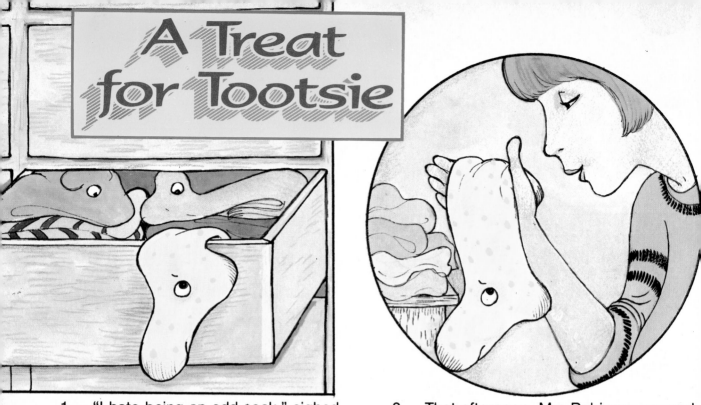

1 — "I hate being an odd sock," sighed Tootsie. "I'm no use for anything!" Tootsie lived in a drawer with the rest of Mr Robinson's socks.

2 — That afternoon, Mrs Robinson opened the drawer. "It's time these socks were tidied. This odd one can go for a start!" Tootsie was thrown on a pile of old clothes.

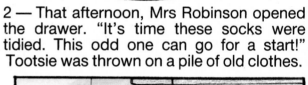

3 — Then Lucy, Mrs Robinson's daughter, spotted Tootsie. "You can't throw this sock out, Mum!" cried Lucy. "I nearly forgot," said Mrs Robinson. "You can take it then."

4 — Lucy pinned Tootsie by the fireplace. Then she went to bed. "Why have I been pinned here?" yawned Tootsie. She was becoming sleepy.

5 — Soon Tootsie fell asleep. The next thing she heard was a noise from the chimney. She felt afraid. "Hello," said a voice. "You must be the Christmas stocking this year."

6 — Suddenly a cheery-faced man in red appeared. "I'm Santa Claus," he said. "And I'm here to deliver Lucy's presents." He began to fill Tootsie with lovely gifts.

7 — Next morning, Lucy ran over to Tootsie and lifted her carefully down from the fireplace. "Look, look, Mummy." she cried. "My stocking's full of presents. I'm glad you didn't throw this sock out."

8 — Tootsie was glad she hadn't been thrown out, too. For only an odd sock can make a proper Christmas stocking!

The King's new castle

KING KINDHEART suited his name. He always made sure that the villagers in Happyland had plenty food and firewood.

One evening, a terrible storm struck Happyland. Rosie Baker and her family sat in their cosy cottage and listened to the thunder.

"Do you think the villagers' homes will be damaged by this storm?" Rosie asked.

"No!" smiled Mrs Baker. "King Kindheart has made our cottages strong and warm."

Sadly, however, King Kindheart couldn't afford to spend money on his own castle, as well as the villagers' cottages. His castle was cold and draughty. Now, the King had caught a bad cold.

The kind King cheered himself up with the thought that the villagers' cottages would be safe and warm, despite the storm.

In the morning, the villagers looked at King Kindheart's castle and gasped in horror.

The wind had smashed the castle's windows and loosened the bricks. There was a hole in the roof and the moat had overflowed.

The King asked Mr Bricks, the builder, for advice.

"I'm afraid your castle will need to be totally re-built," said Mr Bricks.

So, that afternoon, an architect showed King Kindheart some plans for a new castle. The architect's designs were far too big and grand, however. And when the King heard how expensive it would be to build such a fancy castle, he was horrified.

The architect left and King Kindheart sat down in his garden.

"Why can't someone design a plain, little castle for me?" he sighed.

The village children felt sorry for King Kindheart. They decided to cheer him up.

"We'll have a competition for him to judge," said Rosie Baker. "The King enjoys judging contests."

"We'll make it a sand-castle competition in the sand-pit that King Kindheart built, last year," said one boy.

The children worked hard, building lots of beautiful sand-castles. Then King Kindheart arrived to judge them.

"What a wonderful sight!" the King gasped, when he saw the display of sand-castles.

The children's plan had worked. Being a judge for their contest had taken the King's mind off his worries. He looked much happier.

King Kindheart finally chose a small, plain sand-castle as the winner. It was Rosie Baker's castle. She *did* feel proud.

"That's *my* idea of what a perfect castle should look like," laughed King Kindheart. "Small and cosy and not too fussy looking!"

Mr Bricks overheard the King's comment about Rosie's little sand-castle.

"Did you really mean it when you said that was your idea of a perfect castle?" Mr Bricks asked the King.

King Kindheart nodded.

"Then I think I could build a castle just like it for you," grinned Mr Bricks. "I don't need fancy plans to build a simple castle like that."

So Mr Bricks and the villagers began building the new castle the next day.

King Kindheart was thrilled with the finished castle.

"Thank you!" King Kindheart cheered. "My cosy, new home is just what I wanted."

Winter bulbs

WHEN the snow is falling
And days are cold and short,
We sit around the fireside
Without a single thought
For all the frozen winter bulbs
Underneath the ground,
Pushing through the snowdrift
And making not a sound.

But, when the snow has melted
And spring is in the air,
Those winter bulbs will flower
Making colour everywhere.

The yellow of the daffodil,
The tulips, red and white.
The crocus, yellow, white and mauve —
What a splendid sight!

So when the snow is falling
And hands are cold and numb,
Think about those winter bulbs
And the colour that's to come!

Busy Bee

1 — Busy was a little bee who lived in a hive with lots of other bees. When her day's work was done, Busy liked to explore the countryside.

2 — "See you later!" she called to her chums. "Bye, Busy," they replied. "But don't be late back. You know the Queen likes us to go to bed early."

3 — That evening, Busy had lots of exciting things to tell her friends. But the little bees were too tired to listen. "Go to sleep, Busy," they yawned.

4 — Next day, Busy went exploring as usual. She was flying over a garden when she saw some flowers on a window ledge. "They're beautiful!" buzzed Busy.

5 — Busy dived into the flowers and sipped the nectar. "Yum!" she said, and smacked her lips. "Delicious!" But Busy hadn't noticed the lady of the house shutting the window. Poor Busy was trapped.

6 — "I'll never get home now," Busy wailed unhappily. "The Queen will be very cross." Luckily, the lady saw Busy and set her free. "Thank you," buzzed Busy, as she flew home.

7 — When Busy got back to the hive, she found all the bees waiting for her. "I hope I'm not going to be in trouble," she thought.

8 — But Busy needn't have worried. The Queen had a special mission for her. It was to search around the countryside to find the best place to set up a new hive.

9 — "You're the only one who can do the job," smiled the Queen. "Who'd have thought my exploring would make me so important," Busy yawned, that night.

Twinkle's play-time

Lead Paula and Patch through the maze to deliver a Christmas present.

Try to spot six differences between these two pictures of Twinkle and her Christmas cake.

MERRY XMAS

Nurse Nancy is hanging up stockings for her patients. Can you tell which two are exactly alike?

Try to find six Christmas crackers hidden on these two pages.

Benny has a present for each of his toys. Can you tell which present is for which toy?

You can colour this picture of Elfie and his woodland chums, using your paints or crayons.

Sam

SHONA MACGREGOR has a clever sheepdog called Sam. They live on a farm in the Scottish Highlands.

It had snowed heavily in the Highlands.

"Come on, Sam!" cried Shona. "Let's go sledging."

Shona fetched her sledge from the shed and set off across the farmyard.

"Have a nice time!" Mr MacGregor called.

"We will," replied Shona. "Snow is fun."

However, not everyone was enjoying the winter weather. An old lady, called Mrs Blake, who lived near the MacGregors, knocked on her window as Shona and Sam went past her cottage.

"I wonder what Mrs Blake wants?" said Shona.

Shona and Sam soon found out. Mrs Blake was trapped inside her house by a snowdrift. Sam quickly dug away the snow.

2 — Shona and Sam went into Mrs Blake's cottage.

"I don't feel well," Mrs Blake said. "It's the cold. The snow stopped me getting coal from the coal bunker and my house is freezing."

Shona took blankets from a cupboard and wrapped them round Mrs Blake. Then she fetched coal and lit the stove.

"I'll make you some tea while Sam goes for help," Shona said.

Sam raced off towards the ambulance station in the village.

3 — "Hello, Sam," said the ambulance driver, as the sheepdog ran into the station, barking.

"There must be something wrong for you to be here. Well, lead the way."

The clever sheepdog led the ambulance back to Mrs Blake's cottage.

"Well done," the ambulance driver said to Shona. "Your quick thinking has saved Mrs Blake."

"I'm glad," smiled Shona. "Now I'm off sledging."

But Sam had other ideas! He dashed off round the back of the cottage, barking loudly.

"What's wrong now?" cried Shona.

4 — Shona ran after Sam. They found Mrs Blake's goat, Benjy, lying on the ground, bleating weakly.

"Oh, no!" cried Shona. "The cold has made him unwell, too. We'll have to take him to the vet."

Shona lifted Benjy.

"Ooh!" she gasped. "He *is* heavy. I'll never be able to carry him to the vet's, but I don't want to leave him. What can we do?"

Clever Sam knew how to help, however. He raced round to the front of the cottage.

5 — Sam came back, pulling Shona's sledge.

"Of course!" cheered Shona. "Why didn't I think of that!"

Shona settled Benjy on the sledge and set off into the village. Soon they arrived at the vet's surgery. Shona explained what had happened to Mrs Blake and her goat.

"I'll have a look at Benjy," smiled the vet. "You did well to bring him to me."

Benjy just needed food and warmth to make him better.

"We'll look after him at the farm, until Mrs Blake gets home," said Shona.

"Good," replied the vet. "He'll be safe with you."

6 — Mrs Blake returned home in the spring. Shona and Sam were there to welcome her. Benjy was with them, too, of course!

"You must come to tea tomorrow," said Mrs Blake.

Shona and Sam arrived next day to find a roaring fire and the cottage warm and snug.

"Thank you very much for helping me and Benjy," said Mrs Blake.

"That's all right," replied Shona. "But next time it snows, we'll be round sooner to see if you are all right."

"I'm lucky to have you as a neighbour," smiled Mrs Blake.

Egg box fun

Here's a super selection of funny things to make, using cardboard egg boxes. You will need sticky tape, paint and scissors. You may also need elastic, cotton wool, pipecleaners and thread for decoration.

Charlie the clown is easy to make. Cut out two egg sections and place one on top of the other. Use a small piece of sticky tape to hinge one side of the two sections. This will be the back of Charlie's head. Paint a cheerful face and glue on cotton wool hair. If you like, use one of the "bridges", which joins the sections on the box, for a nose.

Use a pair of side by side egg sections to make these funny spectacles. Ask an adult to pierce a hole in both sides of the "spectacles".

Knot and thread a length of elastic — long enough to fit around your head — through both holes. Then paint your spectacles with bright colours.

You can use this shape to make lots of different heads and animals.

Patch pictures

Why don't you try making a "patch picture"? All you need are scraps of fabric, felt, netting, lace trims, wool, buttons, cotton wool, scissors and glue.

Cut pieces of scrap material into different shapes and stick to card to make a picture. You could use buttons for faces, wool for hair, cotton wool for clouds — in fact, anything you like.

The patch picture shown here should give you some ideas. Have fun!

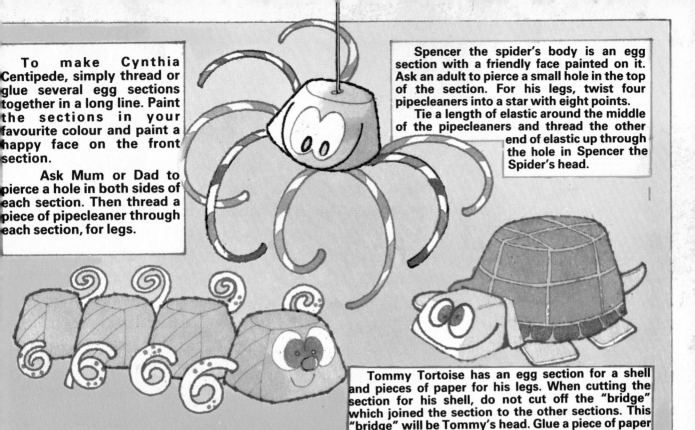

To make Cynthia Centipede, simply thread or glue several egg sections together in a long line. Paint the sections in your favourite colour and paint a happy face on the front section.

Ask Mum or Dad to pierce a hole in both sides of each section. Then thread a piece of pipecleaner through each section, for legs.

Spencer the spider's body is an egg section with a friendly face painted on it. Ask an adult to pierce a small hole in the top of the section. For his legs, twist four pipecleaners into a star with eight points. Tie a length of elastic around the middle of the pipecleaners and thread the other end of elastic up through the hole in Spencer the Spider's head.

Tommy Tortoise has an egg section for a shell and pieces of paper for his legs. When cutting the section for his shell, do not cut off the "bridge" which joined the section to the other sections. This "bridge" will be Tommy's head. Glue a piece of paper over the front of the "bridge" for Tommy's face.

WEE Benny's sweet, but seldom neat,
   He's full of fun and joy.
He's grubby, friendly, naughty, cute,
   Like any little boy. He's ...

My Baby Brother

ON winter mornings, Benny builds
   A jolly man of snow,
Then borrows Dad's old hat and scarf
   To keep him warm, you know!

On winter afternoons we feed
   The ducks. The pond's all ice!
"Quack, quack!" they say. "We're glad you've come.
   This bread is very nice!"

On winter evenings, Benny likes
    A crumpet for his tea.
"And lots of butter on it, please,"
    The rascal says to me.

On winter nights, Ben runs to fetch
    His favourite story book.
I read him tales of long ago
    Beside the chimney nook.

Panto puzzle-time

Colour this picture of Cinderella, with your paints or crayons, then try to find six hidden pots of gold.

A.

B.

C.

Which genie belongs to this lamp?

Answer. B.

Lead Jack through the maze to the Giant's castle.

Try to spot six differences between these two pictures of Dick Whittington.

Cheeky chatterbox

NOW come along to Acorn Wood.
   There's someone you must see.
A certain little chatterbox,
   As cheeky as can be.

His twinkly eyes are quick and bright.
   His coat is russet red.
All day he gathers nuts and fruit
   For winter nights ahead.

He builds his twiggy nest, or drey,
   Among the treetops tall.
And there he's cosy safe, and warm,
   When snow begins to fall.

Tread softly now. He's very shy,
   So don't disturb his play.
For, if you shout and rush about,
   He'll quickly dart away.

Then off he scampers at a dash,
   With goodies for his store.
"Cuck-cuck!" he calls, and, in a flash,
   He scampers back for more.

With tufty ears and bushy tail,
   He is a merry sight.
So, tell me, can you guess his name?
   A squirrel! — Yes, that's right!

Tiger-lion

THERE was great excitement in the little town of Tranton. A new toy shop was just about to open and all sorts of lovely toys were sitting on the shelves.

There were big dolls, baby dolls with pink bows, soldier dolls and all kinds of fluffy toys.

But there was one fluffy toy which did not really look like *anything* at all. He had big, brown eyes, long arms and legs and a very thin, stripy body.

Since he had a face which looked a little bit like a lion and a stripy body, like a tiger, the other toys called him "Tiger-lion".

"Excuse me," said Tiger-lion, one day, to the largest baby doll in the shop. "Can I sit beside you? I want someone to notice me and buy me to take home with them."

"Go away!" said the large doll, in a squeaky voice. "I don't want *you* beside me!"

2 – Poor Tiger-lion felt sad and began to cry big tiger-lion tears which rolled down his button nose, ran along his long whiskers and plopped on to the little clockwork mouse on the floor below him.

Tiger-lion sniffed loudly and dried his eyes on his long, colourful striped arm. The tears made his fur so wet that he felt very uncomfortable. Tiger-lion thought that he could call out to the lions on the shelf above.

"Can you help me up? I'd like to play with you. Catch hold of my arm and pull me up," he called.

"Go away, Tiger-lion!" shouted the smallest lion. "You frighten me with that loud roar of yours. Stay where you are."

So, Tiger-lion wrapped his long, stripy arms around his skinny body, tucked his lanky legs under his chin, and fell fast asleep.

3 – The next thing Tiger-lion knew was that the whole shop seemed to be full of noisy, excited children looking at all the toys on the shelves.

"What a lovely baby doll. She's just what I want for my birthday!" cried one little girl.

"Over here, Mum. Come quickly!" shouted a little boy. "This soldier doll is just what I need to go in my tank."

As the days and weeks went by, most of the new toys in the toy shop had been sold and other toys had been brought in to take their place. When Tiger-lion asked the new toys if he could sit up on the shelf with them, he always got the same reply.

"Go away, Tiger-lion!" they would call. "We don't want to be seen with you. You're too dirty."

It was true. Tiger-lion's stripy body *did* look rather grubby and soon the shop-keeper decided to put him in the bargain basket to be sold at half price.

4 – "Stop shouting, Tiger-lion!" complained the toys. "You'll give us a sore head. Get down to the bottom of the basket!"

"No," said Tiger-lion. "I want everyone to see me."

At that moment, a little boy came running towards the bargain basket. He grabbed Tiger-lion and whirled him round and round his head.

"Look at the funny toy, Mum," the boy shouted.

The toys laughed as poor Tiger-lion went whirling round and round.

The boy's mother made him put Tiger-lion back in the basket. Quickly the other toys heaped themselves all around him and on top of him.

"Maybe now you'll keep quiet and we'll get some peace," they sneered.

5 – "Well," said the shopkeeper, one day, "I think it's time to throw out all the grubby toys from this bargain basket. It looks as if nobody wants to buy this old, stripy lion."

Just at that moment, however, a pretty little girl came into the shop with her mummy. She saw the shopkeeper pulling Tiger-lion out of the bargain basket and went over to have a look.

"Come here, Gwen," called out the girl's mummy. "Come and see these lovely cuddly lions. Would you like one?"

But Gwen was not listening. Gently, she picked up Tiger-lion in her little hands.

"Oh, a Tiger-lion!" she cried with delight. "A Tiger-lion! I must have him."

"She knows my name!" thought Tiger-lion.

"Would you like him?" asked the shopkeeper.

"Oh, yes, please!" cried Gwen. "He's going to be my very special new friend. I love him."

As the girl wound her arms round Tiger-lion, he leaned his large head on her shoulder. Tiger-lion had never been as happy and he grinned from whisker to whisker as he waved "good-bye" to all the other toys in the toy shop.

Silky Suki Siamese

BRIGHT blue eyes and dark brown nose,
    Dark brown tail and dark brown toes.
Coat of palest coffee silk,
    Tiny teeth as white as milk.
Slinky, slender, lightning — quick,
    Watch her do her latest trick.
She has learned to open doors.
    In each corner, she explores.
She likes chicken. She likes fish,
    Served upon her special dish.
She likes playing games with me.
    See her climb the apple tree.
She is always sure to please,
    Silky Suki Siamese.

SUKI

Susie Saucepan

SUSIE SAUCEPAN squeaked unhappily as Mrs Jones unwrapped a shiny, new saucepan and set it on the kitchen shelf.

"Oh, dear!" she sighed. "What will become of me?"

"I'm going to do your job," boasted the new saucepan. "I've heard that you've got a hole in your side. You're no use to anyone now."

Shortly after, Mrs Jones took Susie out of the kitchen and put her in a cupboard under the stairs. Susie did not like it there. It was very dark and lonely, not a bit like her shelf in the nice, warm kitchen.

After a while the cupboard door opened again. It was Mrs Jones.

"At last," thought Susie, "they've decided to get me mended."

But Mrs Jones took the saucepan out into the farmyard and threw it on to a rubbish dump.

"Mr Jones is right," said Mrs Jones. "There's no use keeping broken old pans in the house. They're only fit for the rubbish dump."

"But I could still be a useful saucepan!" cried Susie. "I'll just turn rusty if I lie here."

Then Susie heard a very loud voice.
"Moooooo! Who's making all that noise?" it said.

Susie jumped. Then she looked up. Bending over her was a large, brown cow.

"Hello," said Susie. "I'm looking for a new home. Can you help me?"

The cow thought for a moment.

"Well," she said, "I suppose I could use you as a hat to keep the sun out of my eyes."

Susie was delighted. The cow tossed the saucepan gently in the air, so that it landed in the middle of her head.

But, oh, dear! Every time the cow bent down to eat some grass, Susie fell off.

"It's no good!" exclaimed the cow. "I'm sorry, I can't keep you." She left Susie by the edge of the field.

Susie lay very still. Before long, she heard the rustle bustle of a rabbit.

"Hello," said Susie. "I'm looking for a new job. Could you use me?"

"Goodness me, no," answered the rabbit. "Anyway, I haven't time to stop and chat, because I am on my way to the stream for a drink."

Susie thought very hard. Then her eyes lit up.

"If you take me to your house I can catch the rain and then you won't need to go to the stream to find water."

The rabbit decided this was a splendid idea. He helped Susie back to his burrow and left her outside. Soon it began to rain.

"Now I can show the rabbit how useful I am," Susie thought, feeling very pleased.

When it had stopped raining, the rabbit hopped out of his burrow to have a drink. He was very thirsty. But there was no water to be seen inside Susie at all. It had all fallen through the hole in her side.

"Dear me," sighed the rabbit. "This will never do. You're no use to me." He hopped away to find the stream.

Susie felt very sad. After a while, however, she heard another voice.

Susie smiled when she saw a squirrel.

"Excuse me," she called. "Perhaps I can help you."

The squirrel stopped and blinked.

"A saucepan?" he cried. "Goodness gracious. How can *you* help me?" He scurried towards Susie and peered inside.

"Oh, dear," he began, "dear, dear me."

The squirrel scratched his head, thinking. Then he twitched his tail.

"I have an idea!" he exclaimed. "I'll take you to my house."

The squirrel collected lots of leaves and grass and arranged them inside the little saucepan. When he had finished, he looked very pleased with himself.

"I must go now," he said. "I'll be back soon."

"Whatever can he need me for?" Susie wondered. "I am far too small for him to use as a bed."

Before long, the squirrel returned with his friend, the dormouse. As soon as the dormouse saw Susie he squeaked with delight and excitement.

"Ooooh, thank you, Squirrel!" he cried. "A wonderful new home for the winter."

Susie felt very proud. She would keep the dormouse safe and warm all through the winter. "Now I've got a job to do again," she grinned.

Tabitha

MY pussy cat's called Tabitha.
   I am so fond of her.
Her eyes are green as gooseberries,
   And soft as silk her fur.

I always feed my little cat
   From her own special dish.
She lap, lap, laps the creamy milk,
   And gobbles up the fish.

On sunny days, we have such games,
   Beneath the apple tree.
On winter evenings, how she purrs,
   When snoozing on my knee.

As I race home from school each day,
   She's waiting at the gate.
"Meow!" cries darling Tabitha—
   "About time, too! You're late!"

Becky, Ben and Boots

BECKY and Ben Carter and their Shetland pony, Boots, like to help Mr Carter on his pet stall in the market.

One snowy afternoon, Becky, Ben and Boots were returning home from the market, when Boots became alarmed by a rumbling noise in the distance.

"It's all right, Boots!" laughed Ben. "That's only the gritting lorry spreading sand on the icy roads, to stop cars skidding."

The following day, Becky and Ben decided to clear the snow away from the market stalls. They worked hard, but the ground was still slippery with ice.

Suddenly, Mrs Green, the Carters' neighbour, slipped and fell over. Luckily, she wasn't hurt.

"Other customers might be, however," sighed Mr Carter.

Becky and Ben knew how to solve the problem. They fetched Boots and harnessed him to his cart. Then they visited Mr Parker, the park-keeper.

"Can we use some of the sand from the sand-pit, please?" asked Becky.

"Of course!" smiled Mr Parker.

Becky and Ben filled Boots' cart with sand and hurried back to the market.

Then Boots strolled all around the market place with his loaded cart, while Becky and Ben spread the sand over the ground.

Everyone was very grateful.

"The ground isn't slippery, any more," laughed Becky, "so it's safe to walk on."

"Boots makes a super 'road gritter'," giggled Ben.

When the hutch was open,
On a sunny day,
Ronnie went adventuring,
Dandelion way.

Jane was so unhappy,
When she found he'd fled.
Looked for him all day in
Garden, house and shed.

Then, at last, the neighbour
Called across the wall,
"Here's your Ronnie Rabbit.
He's not lost at all!"

There they found him sitting
In a weedy spot,
Among his favourite dandelions,
Eating up the lot!